SEVEN ATE NINE

Stan Resnicoff

www.StanResnicoff.com

ISBN 978-0-6156-0588-3

The numbers were frantic
All running around

'Cause today number Nine
Was nowhere to be found.

"Call nine-one-one!"
The crowd started to chant

Until someone realized
That without Nine... "we can't!"

The police arrived
Clues found, statements taken

Then all of the numbers
Were marched down to the station.

They paraded the numbers
Out under the lights
And the sergeant proceeded
To read them their rights.

"One of you knows
A lot more than you're saying...
I'll get to the truth
It's no game that I'm playing!"

"It's a lie!" yelled Seven loudly.
"Meant to harm my reputation!"
"I did no such thing inspector,
I was bowling... with the guys-
Four and Eight and Two were there
......we've got airtight alibis!"

They questioned all the numbers
More than you'll ever know,
But they caught nobody lying
So they let the numbers go.

The numbers all were tired
By the time they were released,
But the press just wouldn't let them rest
They'd become... Celebrities!

The interviews were endless,
Some went on Oprah's show
And some of them did Letterman,
Still others, Jay Len-o.

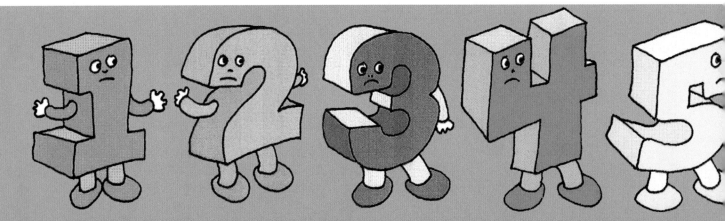

Every number was a big star,
Yet still everybody feared
'Cause no sign of Nine had yet been found.
He had simply... disappeared.

Now everyday just got worse
With no Nine in the system
Everybody came to realize
Just how much they really missed him.

The calendars were worthless
Wall street couldn't sell their stocks
And talk about confusion,
Just look at all those clocks!

Baseball's now eight innings
(And impossible to score)
Prices had to be adjusted
Some got less, and some got more...

Nothing now was working right
No one was having fun
The world was going crazy
Something had to be done!

The inspector then remembered
Something he thought he saw.
"Bring them all back in!", he said
"After all — I am the law."

And when they'd re-assembled
He knew what he had found.
He said "OK Six...... Step forward...
And Six...... please turn around"

Now maybe you were thinking that
No one would ever find him
But as Six began to turn around
There was Nine behind him!

Well they all started yelling
At Nine in all his glory
When six said "Wait — won't you listen
To our side of the story"

"Nine, he was exhausted,
He'd done his very best,
Can't you somehow understand,
He just needed a rest."

"I wanted a safe place
Where you all wouldn't find me,
Then six said "hey — Nine,
Why don't you just get behind me."
It seemed like a good idea at the time,
We both never realized you'd think it's a crime.

"But enough's enough!
Now that I've been discovered
I'm back! I feel great!
I am fully recovered!"

"And besides no harm was done,
And do I need to mention
All the other numbers got
A little extra attention."

Right then the inspector proclaimed,
With a flick of his wrist
"There's no criminal here,
This case is dismissed!"

Well they all started cheering
Together in perfect rhythm
They all were so happy
That Nine was back with them.

They threw a big party
It was not very formal
To celebrate that soon
They'd be back to normal.

And the next day there was
A giant headline
And all it said was (in big letters)...
NINE'S FINE!

Epilogue

The numbers all thought
That Nine was a hero
Back in his place
Between the Eight and the Zero.

The End

Made in the USA
Monee, IL
16 June 2022

98104462R00021